Lucy & Tom's
1 2 3

TED SMART

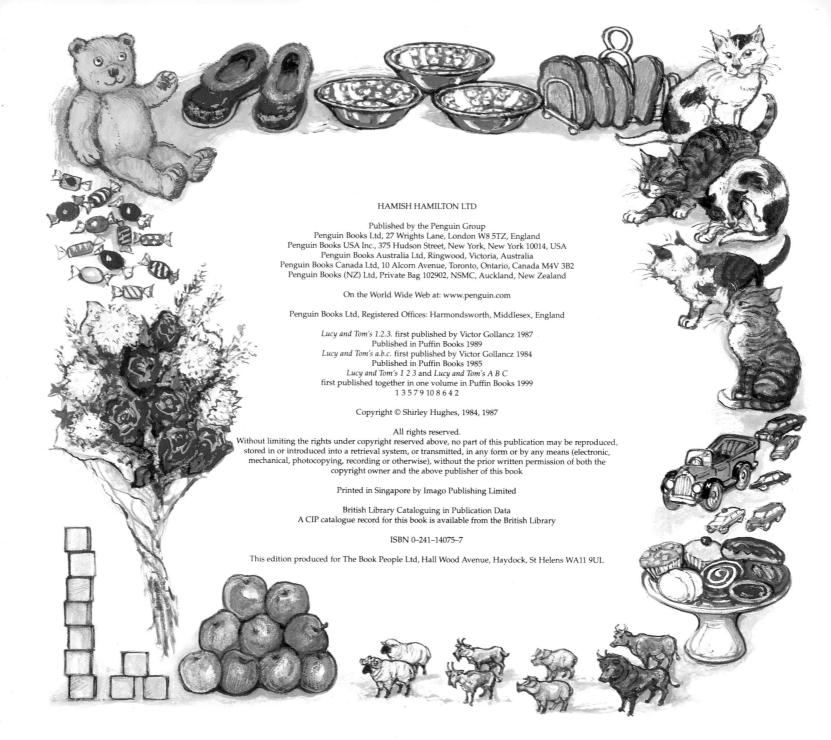

HAMISH HAMILTON LTD

Published by the Penguin Group
Penguin Books Ltd, 27 Wrights Lane, London W8 5TZ, England
Penguin Books USA Inc., 375 Hudson Street, New York, New York 10014, USA
Penguin Books Australia Ltd, Ringwood, Victoria, Australia
Penguin Books Canada Ltd, 10 Alcorn Avenue, Toronto, Ontario, Canada M4V 3B2
Penguin Books (NZ) Ltd, Private Bag 102902, NSMC, Auckland, New Zealand

On the World Wide Web at: www.penguin.com

Penguin Books Ltd, Registered Offices: Harmondsworth, Middlesex, England

Lucy and Tom's 1.2.3. first published by Victor Gollancz 1987
Published in Puffin Books 1989
Lucy and Tom's a.b.c. first published by Victor Gollancz 1984
Published in Puffin Books 1985
Lucy and Tom's 1 2 3 and *Lucy and Tom's A B C*
first published together in one volume in Puffin Books 1999
1 3 5 7 9 10 8 6 4 2

Copyright © Shirley Hughes, 1984, 1987

Printed in Singapore by Imago Publishing Limited

British Library Cataloguing in Publication Data
A CIP catalogue record for this book is available from the British Library

ISBN 0-241-14075-7

This edition produced for The Book People Ltd, Hall Wood Avenue, Haydock, St Helens WA11 9UL

One morning, very early…
one little girl called Lucy fast asleep in bed;
one tousled head cuddled down on the pillow,
one pink nose,
one mouth, a little bit open,
and one very special teddy tucked in beside her.

Lucy's little brother Tom is the first to wake up.
He opens both his eyes wide, jumps out of bed
and tugs at Lucy's quilt. Now there are two children,
wide awake and ready for another day.

It isn't time to get dressed yet but Tom puts on
some woolly socks to keep his toes warm. One is
blue and the other is striped. Not a proper pair,
but never mind.

Lucy's looking for something. She's lost one of
her slippers. Wherever is it? Good, here it is,
under the bed.

Lucy tips all her plastic animals out of their box and she and Tom make them march across the floor, two by two.

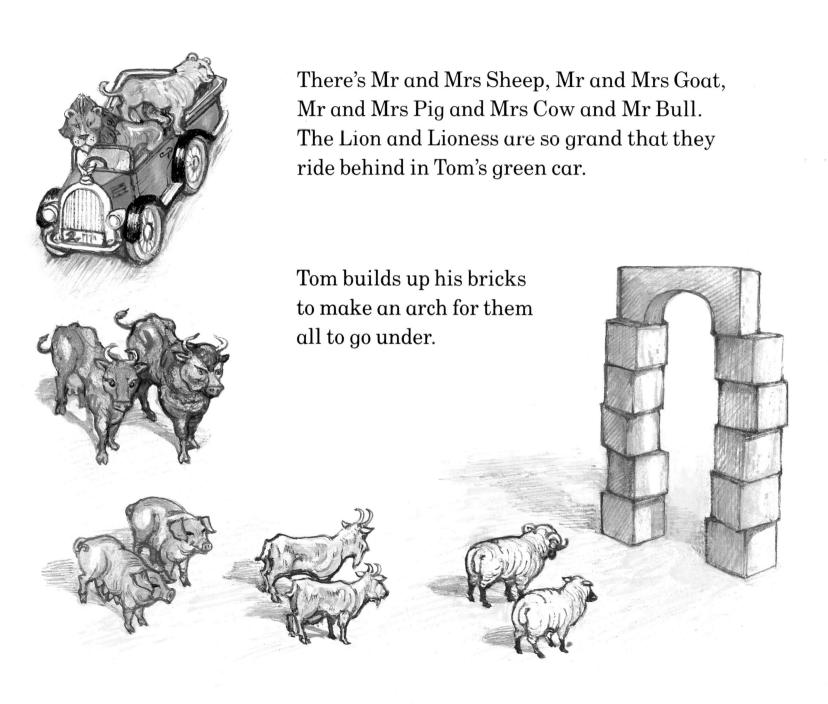

There's Mr and Mrs Sheep, Mr and Mrs Goat,
Mr and Mrs Pig and Mrs Cow and Mr Bull.
The Lion and Lioness are so grand that they
ride behind in Tom's green car.

Tom builds up his bricks
to make an arch for them
all to go under.

Now Dad puts his head round the door and tells
them to come downstairs in their dressing-gowns.
Mum is having a little extra sleep this morning
so there are only three people for breakfast.

Lucy can lay the table: three mugs, three bowls,
three plates and three spoons. Just one knife
for Dad and a little spoon for him to stir his coffee.

Tom watches Dad cut the bread to make toast.
The toaster takes two slices of bread at a time,
so first they make two slices, one each for Lucy and Tom,
then two for Dad. When they are done Tom
arranges all four slices carefully in the toast-rack
and puts them on the table.

Today is Saturday.
No school this morning!
Lucy's clothes are on
the chair in Mum and
Dad's bedroom:
a vest and pants,
a pair of red socks,
a T-shirt with stripes
(first a red stripe,
then a blue one,
then a green),
a skirt and, last of all,
a pair of navy-blue shoes
with red laces.
Lucy can put them all on
by herself, all except for
tying the laces, that is.

Tom can put on his pants, one leg into each hole.
But he needs a bit of help with his sweater. Which
is the way out? It's all dark inside! At last he
finds both the arm-holes and then out pops his head.

As soon as they are dressed Lucy and Tom
go to see how Mopsa the cat is getting on.
A very exciting thing happened a few weeks ago.
Mopsa had kittens! She and her family are
living in a box in the corner of the kitchen.
It's very cosy inside with a bit of Lucy's old
woolly blanket for a bed.

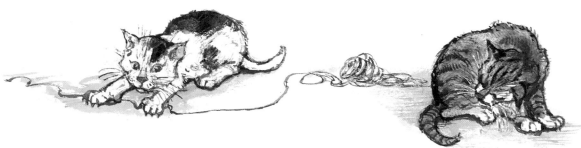

While Mopsa has her breakfast
the kittens come out to play
on the kitchen floor. There are
five of them, but only two are
tabby cats like Mopsa.

They have tiny claws, as many
on each paw as Lucy and Tom
have fingers on one hand, and
they're very sharp too!

Mum says that when the kittens are bigger they'll
be able to keep one and find good homes
for the other four. Lucy and Tom want
to keep them ALL! But six cats are rather
too many for one family.

It's time to go shopping. While Mum and Dad search about for shopping bags and money, Lucy and Tom are all ready and waiting at the gate.

Out in the street there are
lots of things to count. There's
the windows in the house opposite,

the birds sitting on
the telephone wires,

people on the crossing,

and lampposts as far as the corner.

Paving stones are difficult.
They seem to go on for ever!

Number 5   Number 7   Number 9

Lucy and Tom's house is Number 7. Next door on one side is Number 9 and on the other is Number 5. Number 4 , Number 6 and Number 8 are across the street. What a funny way to count. But the postman must get used to it.

Lucy knows that if she and Tom have four sweets,
or six or eight or even ten, they can share them
out equally. But if they have five or seven or
nine sweets they have to cut one of them in half or
else somebody is sure to be cross.
Luckily, today there's no trouble.

At last they are all off to the shops. At the supermarket there are a huge number of things to buy,
rows and rows of them. Tom rides on the trolley and
helps Mum to choose. They take packets and tins
off the shelves and Mum checks them off her
shopping list. Sometimes they come in ones, sometimes
in fours or sixes or even tens and twelves.

Lucy helps Dad to get the fruit and vegetables.
They put them into plastic bags and weigh them
on the scales. Let's see now ... carrots, onions,
tomatoes, oranges; a pound of apples in one bag (only four
because they're quite heavy) and a pound of spinach
leaves in another (lots because they're much lighter).

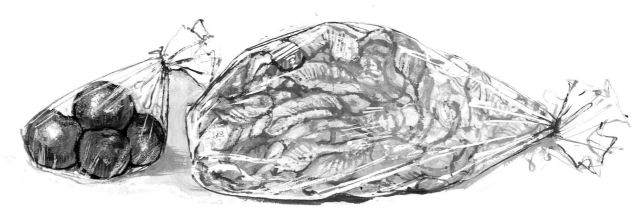

Last of all they buy a big box of chocolates for Granny because it's her birthday today. Also a tube of tiny little sweets, all different colours to decorate her cake. They're called Hundreds and Thousands. There are far too many to count.

Now for the check-out. Everyone stands in line waiting to pay. Dad packs all the things into shopping bags while Mum pays and the lady gives her the change.

On the way home they stop by a flower stall to buy
a bunch of flowers to take to Granny's birthday
tea-party that afternoon. Lucy and Tom help to
choose the colours, six bright red ones and five
creamy white, with some pretty green stuff to
go with them. Won't Granny be pleased?

Home again, Lucy and Tom go into
the back garden to play while Mum
and Dad unpack the shopping. Lucy
decides she will give her two old dolls
a bath in the big washing-up bowl.
It's too heavy to carry out when it's
full of water so Mum gives Lucy a
jug and says that she can fill up
the bath herself from the outside tap.
Lucy has to make a lot of rather drippy
journeys to and fro before it's ready.

Now in go the dolls for a good wash. Little Sophie
floats on the surface, bobbing about with her arms
and legs in the air. Poor Sarah has a hole in her
back. She soon fills up with water and sinks to
the bottom. Lucy has to rescue her and wrap her up
in a bit of towel in case she catches cold.

Tom's making a see-saw. He plays the game of putting
different toys on it to see which one goes up in
the air and which hits the ground.

Sometimes you can get them to balance so that
they're both up in the air at the same time.

When he gets tired of this Lucy helps him to make
a road for the cars to go along. Then Tom makes his
see-saw into a ramp. The cars go shooting down.
They have a race to see which car shoots
off furthest at the bottom. The big green
car wins. Then it's time for lunch.

After lunch Mum and Dad want to sit down for
a while before it's time to go to Granny and Grandpa's.
Mum gives Tom and Lucy a piece of paper each
to make birthday cards.

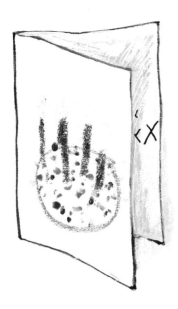

Tom folds his paper in half, like this. On the front he draws a picture of a big birthday cake with candles and lots of coloured dots all over it (those are the Hundreds and Thousands). Inside he writes his name and puts ten kisses.

Tom xxxxx
xxxxx

Lucy folds her paper in half and then in half again. It looks smaller than Tom's. There's just room on the front to draw a picture of a bunch of flowers. But when you open it up, the back looks like this:

xxxx
love
from
Lucy

At last it's time to go to Granny's tea-party.
Granny is sixty today. She's very pleased with
her flowers and chocolates, and with Lucy and
Tom's cards which she puts on the mantelpiece
for everyone to see.

There's a very special tea with sandwiches,
biscuits, fancy pastries and a lovely big birthday
cake.

Granny says that she can't possibly blow
out her candles all by herself so Lucy and
Tom have to help her.

One, two, three, BLOW!
Happy Birthday, Granny!
Well done, Lucy and Tom!

Lucy & Tom's
A B C

A   Lucy and Tom know a lot of words beginning
with **a**. **a** is for **a**pples and **a**nts, also for **a**pricots,
aunties, **a**eroplanes, **a**crobats and **a**rtists.   **a**

b is for **b**ooks and **b**ed. Lucy and Tom nearly always have a story read to them at bedtime. Tom knows most of his favourite stories by heart. When he's in bed he can look at the pictures and read aloud to himself. Lucy keeps some of her special books under her pillow, just in case.

B

b

C

c is for **C**ats, of course. Lucy and Tom's cat is called Mopsa. Her fur is brown with black stripes and patches of white. She doesn't often get cross or scratchy unless she's playcd with for just a bit too long.

C

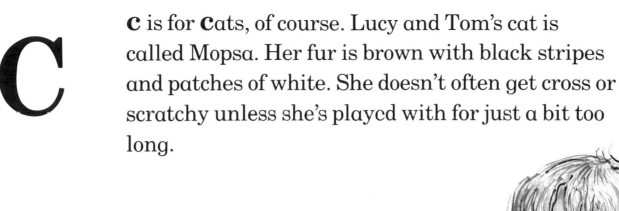

c is for **C**olours and **C**rayons too. It's fun mixing up the colours to make different ones.

D **d**

d is for dogs. There are four living in Lucy and Tom's street. A little fluffy one, two middle-sized ones, and a big spotted one called Duchess. Tom doesn't like Duchess very much because she keeps knocking him over.

d is also for ducks who live on the lake in the park. Lucy and Tom often take them some bits of bread in a paper-bag, and they come waddling up out of the water to be fed.

E e

e is for **e**ggs, chocolate ones at Easter, all wrapped up in shiny paper, and real ones for breakfast. Lucy and Tom sometimes play a trick on Dad by putting an empty egg-shell upside down in his egg-cup. When he taps it, there's nothing inside. What a horrible surprise!

f is for **f**riends. Lucy's best friend is Jane. They are in the same class at school and see each other every day. Tom's friends are James and Sam. They often play together. Sometimes they get cross with each other, but friends are important people so you can't be cross for long.

F   f

G g

G is for **G**ranny and **G**randpa, two other very important people.

There are plenty of interesting things to do at Granny and Grandpa's house. Lucy helps Granny in the garden and Tom helps Grandpa mend things. They have some long talks together.

H

h is for **h**omes and **h**ouses.

Can you see where Lucy and Tom live?

h

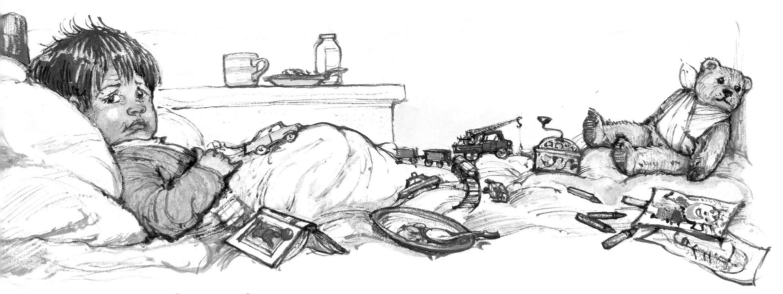

i is for **i**ll. This is Tom being ill in bed. He needs
a lot of things to play with. Even then, he gets very
hot and bored and keeps calling out for people to
come and amuse him. Lucy is only a little bit ill.
She's on the sofa, eating ice-cream.

I

i

J j

j is for **j**umping. Lucy has a skipping-rope and she's learning to skip. She can get up to ten or even more. Tom can jump from the second stair, and from one paving stone to another. Sometimes he jumps on the furniture, too, though it's not really allowed.

K

k is for **k**ites, flying high up over the windy hill.

k

L l

l is for **l**ight. There's sunlight, torchlight and twilight. There are street-lights, car-lights and the fairy-lights on the Christmas tree. And there's the light that shines in from the landing when Lucy and Tom are asleep.

M

m is for **m**oon, the most magic light of all.

m

N

n is for **n**ursery school, where Tom spends
his mornings.

n

O

O is for **O**ranges and **O**range-juice, which you can suck through a straw. **O** is also for **O**ven. There are some good smells coming out of this one, but you have to be careful because it's VERY HOT.

P

p is for **p**ark and **p**laying.

p

Q

q is for **q**ueens, which is one of Lucy and Jane's favourite games. Tom is supposed to hold up their trains, but he doesn't often want to.

q

R

r is for **r**ooms. These are some of the rooms in Lucy and Tom's house.

r

S   S

S is for **S**treets and **S**hops, Lucy and Tom have been to the supermarket with Mum. They've bought something else beginning with **S**. Can you guess what it is?

T  **t**

t is for **t**oys, **t**eatime and **t**elevision.

U

u

u is for **u**mbrellas.

V v

v is for **V**oices. You can whisper in a very soft, tiny voice, like this, or you can shout in a VERY LOUD, NOISY VOICE, LIKE THIS, or you can make music with your voice by singing a tune. There are cross voices and kind voices, high voices and deep voices, happy voices and whiney voices. Which kind of voice do you like best?

W is for **W**inter when it's too cold to play outside.
The windows have frost on them and the water
is frozen over.

When the snow comes, all the world is white.

X **X**

X is for **X**ylophone. Lucy's xylophone has eight notes and each one makes a different sound when you strike it. You write notes in a special way, like this:

Y

y is for **y**achts on the water and **y**achtsmen on the shore.

y

Z

z is for **Z**oo, of course.

Z

Z is also the end of the alphabet, and
this is the end of Lucy and Tom's **a.b.c.**

AaBbCcDdEeFfGgHhIiJjKkLlMmNnOoPpQqRrSsTtUuVvWwXxYyZz